I0749224

ON BACKGAMMON TIME

TAHIR SHAH

MARIANA GARCIA PIZA

ON BACKGAMMON TIME

TAHIR SHAH

MARIANA GARCIA PIZA

MMXXIII

Secretum Mundi Publishing Ltd
124 City Road
London
EC1V 2NX
United Kingdom

www.secretum-mundi.com
info@secretum-mundi.com

First published by Secretum Mundi Publishing Ltd in
Daydreams of an Octopus & Other Stories, 2022
Published in this edition, 2023

ON BACKGAMMON TIME

Artwork drawn by Mariana Garcia Piza

A CIP catalogue record for this title is available from the British Library.

ISBN 978-1-914960-91-8

VERSION 05092023

Visit the author's website:
Tahirshah.com

I imagine that the title of this
tale means nothing to you.

After all, how could you have
heard of such a curious thing?

There was a time when I was as you are now, unknowing and raw…

...a time when I had not ventured
to the Land of Grosticam.

On another evening I will regale you with tales of my wider adventure, and explain how the curse that now afflicts me was meted out there.

But, for now, I would like to offer an episode that was quite unlike anything that had occurred in my life until that time.

It centred around my love for backgammon.

You see, I come from a family of traders…

...the kind who spend their lives
in the old cities of the East.

They while away the hours, waiting for buyers to peruse their wares.

But such is life, and customers
are few and far between.

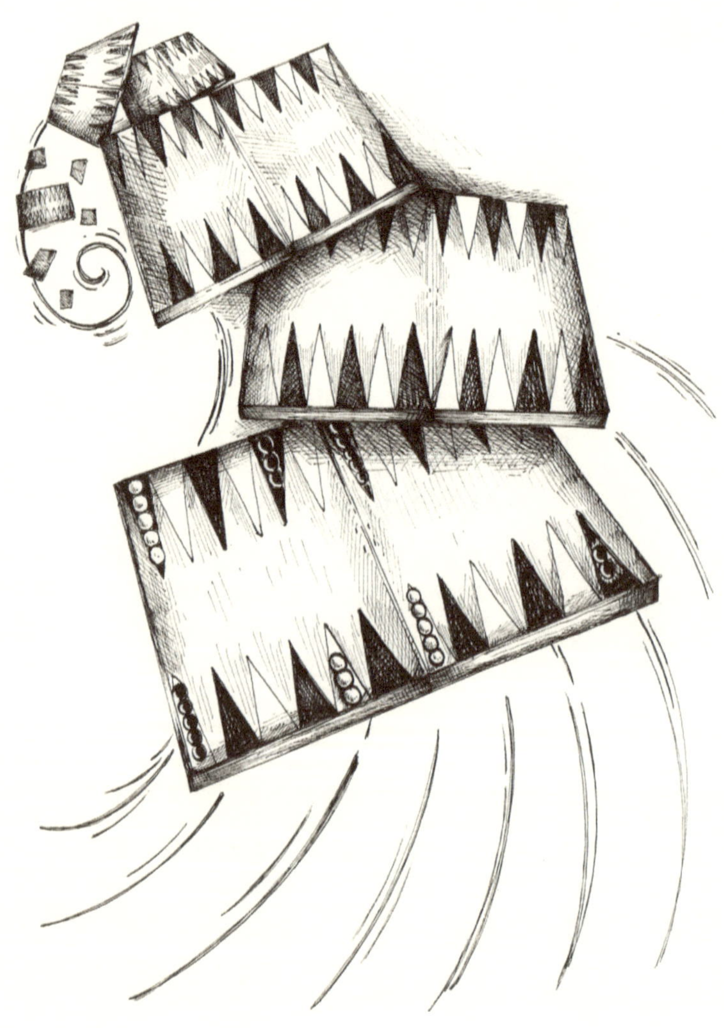

And that means one thing: a life of sweet mint tea, stories, and endless games of backgammon.

When youth had drained away into adulthood,
my father pointed at me, then at the horizon.

‘You are to go on a journey,’ he said.

‘Why, Baba?’ I answered.

‘Because you are far too clean and comfortable, and because if you are to succeed in life you will need hands far less smooth than you now have.’

‘Where should I go?’ I asked.

My father balked at the question. 'Anywhere... but only come back when what you take for certainty has been changed by experience.'

At dawn the next morning I set off and, after a litany of adventures, reached the ancient crumbling walls of that desert outpost – the Land of Grosticam.

At first glance there was nothing especially unusual about it. The buildings were made from stone hewn from the nearby mountains which circled the plain.

The bazaar was packed with the kind of wares found in such places, drawn from all corners of the compass.

There were heaps of ripe pomegranates and melons as fine as any I'd ever seen, baskets woven by prisoners in the next kingdom, and all manner of magical supplies, including blocks of sulphur and antimony.

Above the great bazaar, perched
atop the city wall, was a teahouse.

By day and by night, a riotous miscellany of characters dwelt there, as though washed up by a freak wave of adventure.

Most of them appeared to be fugitives, thieves, or liars. I was careful not to have anything to do with any of them.

But something stirred in me.

It seemed as if I might at last be nearing the answer to the riddle my father had set me.

The day after my arrival, I noticed an elderly man seated alone in the corner of the teahouse.

He had wizened features, but a distinguished countenance. It appeared that he had been born of good blood but had fallen on hard times.

His only possession was a magnificent antique backgammon set. To my surprise, no one ever challenged him to a game.

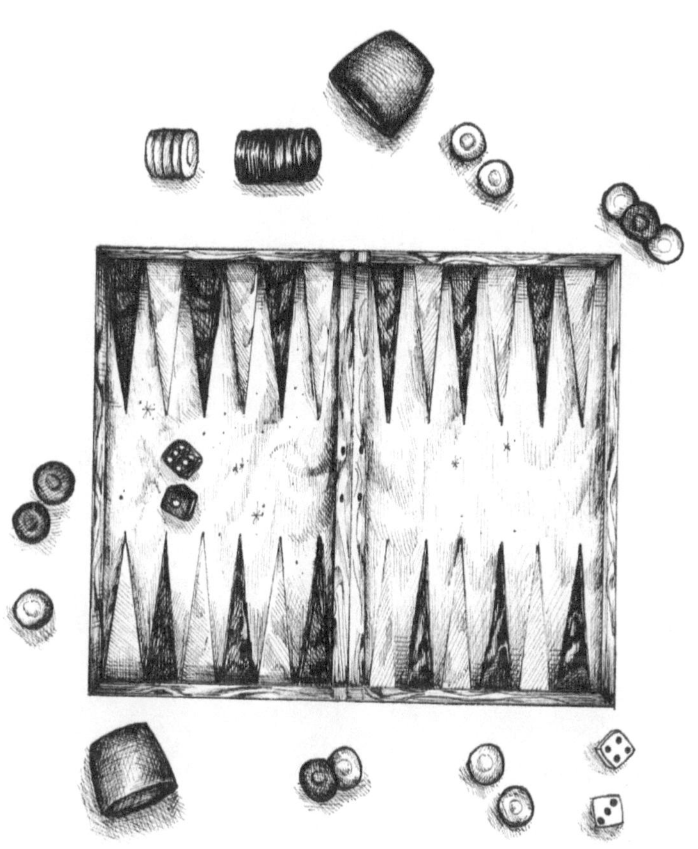

It being such an exquisite board, inlaid with fragments of mother of pearl, I went over and introduced myself.

The next thing I knew, I was seated across from the man, a shaker in my hand.

Before rolling to ascertain who was to take black and who was to take white, I asked whether we were playing for money.

For, even in the bazaars of my own land,
the merchants wagered a small amount
so as to make it a little more exciting.

The wizened owner of the backgammon set ran the side of his hand down his long nose, like a bird preening a wing.

'In Grosticam we do not play for coinage,' he answered. 'Rather, we play for a different kind of currency.'

Frowning, I managed half a smile.
'I don't understand,' I said.

The ancient sniffed hard,
his nostrils distending.

‘We play for time,’ he said.

I did not understand. But, imbued with youthful enthusiasm, I shrugged.

‘Sounds as good a currency as any to me,’
I riposted.

And with that, I shook the dice,
and so did he.

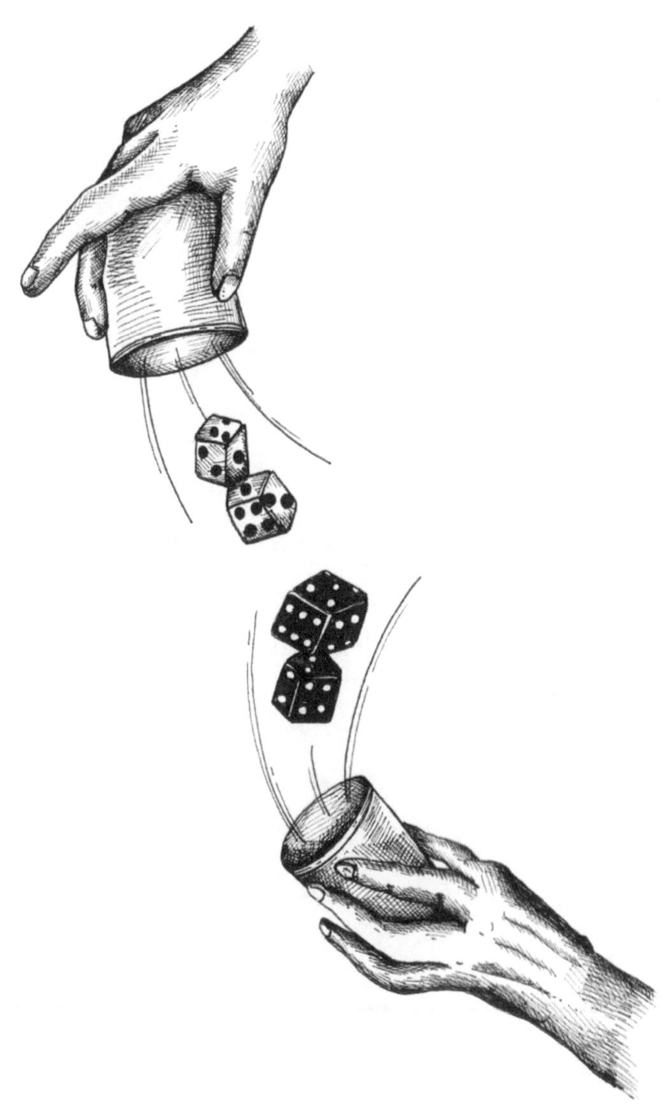

A youth spent in the bazaars of my own country had, I mused, afforded me a clear advantage.

For, right from the start,
I dominated.

The game was going so well for me that
at one stage I even apologized.

My aged opponent said nothing;
he simply smiled wryly to himself.

A little time after the first game had begun,
my run of luck with the dice turned.

It was as though they were against me.

However devious my play, I didn't get
the numbers I needed and, to my despair,
the first game went to him.

As I bemoaned my loss, slapping a hand playfully to my knee, something happened that took me by surprise… something that caused me to shake right down to the bone.

You see, as I conceded defeat,
I felt myself age by a decade.

And, at the same moment, my challenger appeared ten years younger than he had moments before.

I frowned and cursed.

He smiled.

‘What just happened?’ I asked quickly.
‘Time,’ uttered my opponent.

'You mean…?'
'Time slipped away from you
and came to me.'

I swallowed hard.
'But how could such a
monstrous thing take place?!'

The man across from me smiled again.
His skin was brighter, his eyes less sagged.

‘By the magic of the board,’ he said.

'You mean that ten years of my life have been stolen from me?!' I cried.

'No, no,' the player corrected, 'they have not been stolen from you. They have been *won* from you.'

Perspiration ran down my face
as my mind turned in horror.

What was I to do…?

Play on, and risk losing more time
while rejuvenating my adversary?

Or leave now and return home older and
more ripened than I would have wished?

Chilled with fear, I agreed to a second game.

I would stop at nothing until I had defeated him, drawing on the tactics I'd seen used in the bazaars of my home town.

So, we played again.

This time, he went first,
and got a streak of good dice.

But then, as so often happens,
the numbers changed in my favour.

I was drenched in sweat, but my opponent was calm as calm could be. I found this remarkable, as though he were unfazed by the thought of losing his recent gains.

The game went on and on, each one of us playing more brilliantly than I have ever seen.

The ancient, who of course was no longer quite so aged, had a mastery that impressed me greatly.

But as we reached the end of the match,
it was I who trounced him.

‘*Hah*!’
I exclaimed in the most spirited
voice ever to have left my lungs.

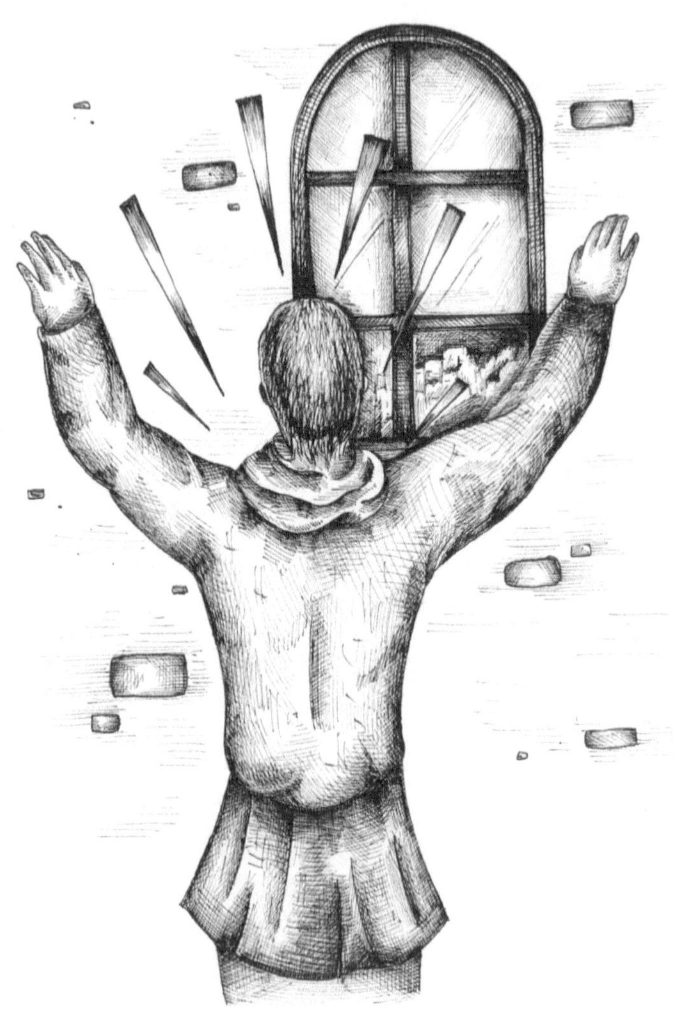

As the sound drifted out through the open
window and over the old city of Grosticam,
I felt every day of the lost decade return.

At the same time, my adversary's appearance was as aged as it had been when I first challenged him.

As soon as the second game was over,
I shook his hand and expressed my sincerest
gratitude for the most enlivening and
dangerous of afternoons.

'I do not wish to appear impolite,' I said, 'but, after all, an elderly gentleman such as yourself has already enjoyed a long life and, I hope, a happy one.'

The man looked at me,
his eyes glazed over with cataracts.

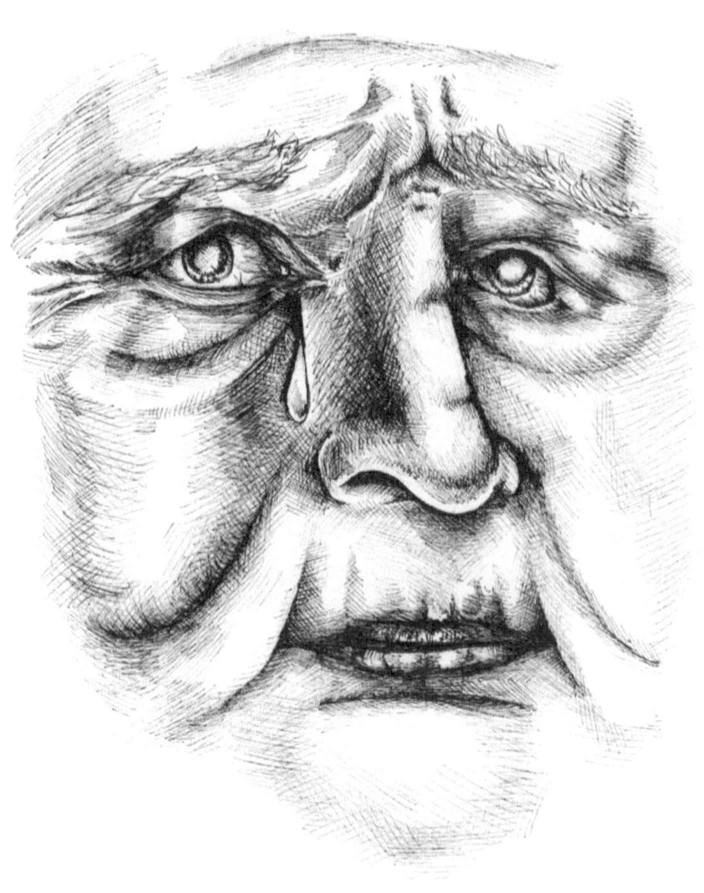

A single tear welled in his left eye and ran down the length of his cheek, the skin of his face wrinkled like elephant hide.

‘Might I enquire your age?’ he said.

I told him.
'I'm twenty.'

The ancient sniffed again,
as though greatly troubled.

'I am the same age as you,' he said.

My gaze roamed from his face down
onto the board, that damned backgammon
board, the one that controlled the
currency of life and death.

‘I am *so* sorry,’ I whispered.

And with that, I left the teahouse,
my head hung low in gratitude and in shame.

Returning to my father's mountainside,
I told the story of Grosticam.

When the last word had left my mouth, I said: 'Baba, when I embarked from this hillside, I believed that a day lived was a day imprinted onto my soul. But now that I have experienced that wretched board, I can never again take time for granted.

'After all, whatever we believe it to be,
time is quite evidently not what it would seem.'

Finis

About the Author

Descended from a long line of storytellers, writers, and savants, Tahir Shah is one of the most prolific authors of his generation. He has published more than sixty books in numerous genres, including travel, fiction, and fantasy, as well as tales for children.

Raised in the tradition of Eastern 'teaching stories', Shah is passionate about stories and storytelling. He regards the ability to learn from folklore as being in us all, what he calls a 'default setting of humankind'. As well as having written scores of books, Shah has made documentaries for National Geographic TV and The History Channel. He is the founder and CEO of the charity, The Scheherazade Foundation.

About the Artist

Mariana Garcia Piza is an educator and illustrator born in Mexico. She started her career as a freelance illustrator in 2016 with a focus on children's books, and has been published across print and web media. She uses both digital and traditional mediums, favouring ink and watercolour vintage illustrations.

Books By Tahir Shah

Travel

Trail of Feathers
Travels With Myself
Beyond the Devil's Teeth
In Search of King Solomon's Mines
House of the Tiger King
In Arabian Nights
The Caliph's House
Sorcerer's Apprentice
Journey Through Namibia

Novels

Jinn Hunter: Book One – The Prism
Jinn Hunter: Book Two – The Jinnslayer
Jinn Hunter: Book Three – The Perplexity
Hannibal Fogg and the Supreme Secret of Man
Hannibal Fogg and the Codex Cartographica
Casablanca Blues
Eye Spy
Godman
Paris Syndrome
Timbuctoo

Nasrudin

Travels With Nasrudin
The Misadventures of the Mystifying Nasrudin
The Peregrinations of the Perplexing Nasrudin
The Voyages and Vicissitudes of Nasrudin
Nasrudin in the Land of Fools

Teaching Stories

The Arabian Nights Adventures
Scorpion Soup
Tales Told to a Melon
The Afghan Notebook
The Caravanserai Stories
Ghoul Brothers
Hourglass
Imaginist
Jinn's Treasure
Jinnlore
Mellified Man
Skeleton Island
Wellspring
When the Sun Forgot to Rise
Outrunning the Reaper
The Cap of Invisibility
On Backgammon Time
The Wondrous Seed
The Paradise Tree
Mouse House
The Hoopoe's Flight
The Old Wind
A Treasury of Tales
Daydreams of an Octopus & Other Stories

Miscellaneous

The Reason to Write
Zigzag Think
Being Myself

Research

Cultural Research

The Middle East Bedside Book

Three Essays

Anthologies

The Anthologies

The Clockmaker's Box

The Tahir Shah Fiction Reader

The Tahir Shah Travel Reader

Edited by

Congress With a Crocodile

A Son of a Son, Volume I

A Son of a Son, Volume II

Screenplays

Casablanca Blues: The Screenplay

Timbuctoo: The Screenplay

A REQUEST

If you enjoyed this book, please review it on your favourite online retailer or review website.

Reviews are an author's best friend.

To stay in touch with Tahir Shah, and to hear about his upcoming releases before anyone else, please sign up for his mailing list:

 http://tahirshah.com/newsletter

And to follow him on social media, please go to any of the following links:

 http://www.twitter.com/humanstew

 @tahirshah999

 http://www.facebook.com/TahirShahAuthor

 http://www.youtube.com/user/tahirshah999

 http://www.pinterest.com/tahirshah

 https://www.goodreads.com/tahirshahauthor

http://www.tahirshah.com

www.ingramcontent.com/pod-product-compliance
Lightning Source LLC
Chambersburg PA
CBHW030522310726
48979CB00010B/1770/J

* 9 7 8 1 9 1 4 9 6 0 9 1 8 *